THE HOUSE ON CHURCH STREET

Randy R. Ervin

PublishAmerica

Baltimore

First printing

ISBN: 1-4137-2007-2
PUBLISHED BY PUBLISHAMERICA, LLLP
www.publishamerica.com
Baltimore

Printed in the United States of America

Contents

Acknowledgments

I would like to thank the following people who helped me put this story together. The thanks for all the ground work, preparation, and many hours goes to Jan Fresorger and her husband Leon Fresorger for his support. Thanks to Elaine Kraska for helping me with a lot of the setup and structure, to Natasha Wescoat, my daughter, for her help with the excellent design of the front cover. I also want to thank Malisa Dobbler and Jim Balenger for their help with the structure of the story, and Judy Troxell for her support of this story, and for allowing this story to be told.

Foreword

This is in loving memory of my Mother, Bunny Troxell, who has gone on to be with the Lord. Her surviving children are Leland, Kevin, Shelly, Kathy, Tammy, Becky, and I. We all miss you, Mom, so much, and we love you.

Introduction

This story is based on my own experience as I was being led into the world of the supernatural, and the concrete steps I took in order to be set free.

The names of the characters and the business in this story have been changed to protect their identity. I would like to make it known that the self-proclaimed white witch that practices witchcraft in this story does not necessarily portray the common practices of all witches.

The History Behind
"The House On Church Street"

Many years ago, my dad purchased an old house that was estimated to be about 100 years old. While digging underneath the house in preparation to level it with jacks, he stumbled upon bones. After a little thought and some dismay, he determined that the bones appeared to be in human form. He was very upset and dumbfounded by this discovery. Still in shock and disbelief, he turned the bones over to an unknown official to be tested. Later, he was told that the bones had been from the body of a Native American and that there could be more bones under the house. They believed that my dad may have discovered a Native American burial ground. At that time no one seemed concerned, as Michigan was known to have Native American burial sites state-wide. My dad did not wish to disturb the burial ground any more than he already had. He placed the bones back under the house and buried them in the same spot he had found them. He did not continue to investigate, hoping he had not disturbed any Spirits that were at rest or protecting the burial ground. This topic was discussed time and again throughout family generations. Many burial grounds in the state of Michigan were thought to have had curses placed on them by the Native Americans years ago for protection against intruders.

While researching for my book years later, I searched for a reason for the horrifying intensity of my encounter with the supernatural. I began to collect as much data as I could find. At the local area Pinconning Library, I discovered an interesting book about the area's Native American villages. The Arenac County historian at the time was Calvin Ennes, the author of the document titled *History of Arenac County, Michigan*. The document is a 200-year genealogy of the Arenac County glossary of several Native Americans. This placed several tribes somewhere within the towns of Sterling and Augres and the city of Standish over many hundred years, although their exact location was unknown. The water shoreline at that time would have brought some of their villages into the city of Standish today.

A Shaman is a term for an Indian holy man, basically a spiritualist (medium), who would communicate with the spirit world. They believed that there were good and evil spirits dwelling in the spiritual realm.

One unknown tribe shaman was known to intercede with the spirits called "The False Faces" (they would carve an image of a distorted face from a living tree, cut a long strand of hair from the tail of a horse, and attach it to the back of the faces). They would dance around the sacred fire while wearing these wooden faces as masks to summon these spirits to come forth. When these distorted bodiless beings appeared, they would be sent to haunt and terrorize the enemy villages throughout the surrounding areas and anyone else who would get in their way.

Today, this area is known as the city of Standish, Michigan.

Chapter One

The Nightmare Begins

In September of 1974 I was 22 years old and living in a small town called Pinconning, about 150 miles north of Detroit, Michigan. I lived about three miles out of town with my Aunt and Uncle. I worked in Standish, in a small shop 12 miles north of Pinconning. I was a wire welder on first shift. My life took me down several turns, all leading to one narrow path, deeper and deeper into a world I could not escape.

Often, my mom would leave her horoscope books lying on the coffee table. I could not resist picking them up to read the contents because I began developing a desire for them. I found out that, being born in December, I was a Sagittarius but a borderline Capricorn since my birthday was on the 21st. The horoscope books told a lot of true things about me and stated that my destiny was drawing me places.

I loved reading my horoscope whenever I could. Horoscopes really got their hooks into me. The books told me many personal things that no one else knew about me. It told me of my weaknesses, strengths, the things that could hurt me, and why I responded to different people the way I did. Man, I was impressed. I was even instructed about how to get along with certain people of other Astrological signs. I kept feeding myself with more and more books on these topics over the months to come. I worked hard at trying to find out more about myself—who I really was and where I was going in life. I kept up on my daily forecast to keep in touch with any updates. Only 50% of these forecasts would actually come true, but I still enjoyed it. I felt so empty inside. What was the real reason I was here on this earth? There must be more to life then this.

What happens after death? I grew up a Methodist, but I only went to church when I was younger. I went to bible school with my grandmother, who also was a Methodist. When I was very young, I often asked myself, "Is God dead?" So many people believe he doesn't exist. I asked myself, "Does he?" many times growing up. In church, there was always this big cross on the wall with this man on it. It caught my attention many times and I would ask myself, "Who is that guy hanging up there on the wall on those pieces of wood?" What did it represent? Why would someone do that? I had a lot of questions that were unanswered.

I was doing okay in my Aunt and Uncle's home. They had six kids, but we all got along together just fine. It was a tight fit for everyone to live there. My uncle, Bud, worked for the Bay County Road Commission, and drove a road grader most of the time, cleaning back roads. My aunt Beth was a school bus driver during the day. She would come home afterwards, take care of her house and the family. Most of the kids would go off to school. The two older boys would work after school. Larry went to work at his new job with GM. Terry had a job also, at the local Pinconning Cheese Store. I shared a bed in the room with my cousin Terry.

That's kind of how my story starts—it was from here that I was introduced by Terry to Pete's Restaurant, and started making new friends. Terry and I checked out the new restaurant in town one day. There were a few pretty waitresses who worked there that kind of drew me in also. Over the weeks to come, it turned out to be like the weekly TV show *Happy Days*: where the young crowd hangs out. We had a pool table and a jukebox in a room where the young crowd hung out and had lots if fun. These were the greatest of times of my life at Pete's Restaurant. We would usually eat and play pool or go partying afterwards. While I got acquainted with the place, I gained some new friends. Terry didn't approve of some of the friends I was hanging out with. He just stopped hanging around after a while. But they soon took me down another path from which I was not going to return. I was introduced to drugs later on. It happened kind of against my will, you could say. One of my new-found friends thought it would be very funny to drop some mescaline in the coffee that I was drinking, and I was not aware of it until about an hour later. I started feeling very funny and started hallucinating. But it wasn't really anything that was scary or terrifying. It actually was very fun. It rescued me from reality at the time and it was something I really liked after a while. Yes, of course I was very ticked off at him for slipping something in my coffee. I chewed him out, only to start laughing uncontrollably. So, I lost that fight. The lack of fear took over, and it became a fun thing. The fear of things cooled off after awhile, and I had an open mind about drugs and smoking pot. It took me into another world for about three years.

I was still so very empty inside. No matter what I tried to fill that void, the excitement would only last a short time. What was my destiny?

Two Months Later

I accepted a new job, driving a two-ton truck for the owner of Pete's Restaurant. I picked up the U.S. Mail at several post offices in the area, from Roscommon to Saginaw. This was the route I traveled four times a week. We had to sleep over in a small room that my boss rented for us in Roscommon as a layover until the afternoon of the next day. Around 6:00 p.m., the drivers would meet at Pete's Restaurant on their way down from up north. We would switch drivers and head for Saginaw. Throughout the day, we dropped off the load that was picked up, reloaded the mail in Saginaw and took it to Lansing. Before I re-loaded the truck, I usually had a two-hour layover. I would often go some where and eat and find something else to do with the rest of my time.

Many times after eating, I would walk through a local mall and stroll through some of the stores. I wasn't much of a reader, but I did like reading books about the supernatural, ghosts stories, haunted houses—you name it, if it was scary I would read it. If it was a movie I would go and watch it. I had been working for the company now almost two years. One cold, gusty day I happened across a book while walking and browsing the book store, specifically looking for my weekly issue of *Astrology*. As I was reaching for my weekly issue, I was immediately drawn to this mysterious-looking book titled *Witchcraft and Your Destiny*. It held a powerful supernatural attraction. The word "destiny" was the key word that struck my attention. I had been trying very hard to find just that for years! My destiny…

Chapter Two

Introduction To The Supernatural

I found the book to be very fascinating. It had all sorts of things that a person could do. It told about the different charms that would bring good luck. I could mend a broken relationship and bring a couple back together. I could even make someone love me beyond their control. Now that would have to be seen! I thought to myself as I laughed. "What else can this book do for me? Hmm. Wow, I can cast spells on people, cause pain and suffering. "Let's see, who do I hate the most? Well, I should save that for later, eh?" There was a chapter on how to speak to the spirit world and contact someone in the spirit realm to locate hidden treasure.

I desperately wanted to buy this one. I rushed out of the mall, went to my truck, and started reading as much as I could before I had to go back to the post office. "Okay, " I said as I paused to look around. I wanted to make sure no one was watching me. I didn't want anyone to come around the truck and cause any interruptions either. "This is a very interesting chapter," I thought to myself. I was just flipping through the pages, reading, when I came across "How to make your dreams and wishes come true." This was exactly what I wanted. I also found "How to find hidden treasures buried in the ground."

"Wow!" I could handle that one.

"Just imagine what I would do if I could find all of the buried money in Arenac County. I could be rich! It says here all I have to do is pick a night when the moon is full. Find a place where I can concentrate, with no noise in the house, and have no one around. I know just the place to go. I'll go to my Dad's house in Standish, yeah, that's a good place. As a matter of fact, I planned on renting this place from him too. I'll just have to pick a night I can do this." So I put the book up and headed back to the post office. I pulled in and backed up my truck to the loading dock to begin loading my truck. All I could do that night was think about that book. The supernatural had always intrigued me for years. There were a lot of superstitious stories in my family that were passed down through generations. There was always one story after another told as I grew up. Stories of omens and premonitions were common in our family. It was a common practice to hear of a relative that had passed away to visit someone in the family, making a quick appearance only to warn of immediate danger. They spoke, guided, and warned us of the present and of the future in many ways. So I was very captivated and excited when I was drawn to this book of the supernatural. There were stories of people walking through a house with their head under their arm. "Yeah, that was a good one. I could go on and on, but if I do I'll scare myself, so I better shut up!" I thought to myself.

I kind of forgot about the book after a few days or so. I was preoccupied by moving into my dad's house that I was to be renting from him. It took me several days moving in my furniture getting the things I needed and setting up everything in its place. I never completely forgot about the book. It was still on my priority list, waiting for the right time to set down and really dig into it. Two weeks later, I was riding around with a friend and we had just smoked a joint of marijuana. I was very high. We drove around for a while and listened to some music, but he had to do something at home. I told him to drop me off at the house so I could finish unpacking.

I entered the house and thought, "I'll bet the best time of all would be tonight to do something with that book I bought. Seeing that I'm still high from being with one of my friends, I thought to myself that this would add to my concentration. So this night should be perfect. I don't have the faintest idea if the moon is out or not—it suggests there be one. Let's just see if this junk works or not."

I was the only one that was present in the house. So I got the book out and starting reading some background on what I was supposed to do. I opened and started reading the book. It instructed me to contact spirits from the spirit world. I was mumbling to myself some names I could not even pronounce. "I wonder if they will come if I can't even pronounce their names correctly? Oh boy, this stuff isn't going to work! I'll at least try it until I get it right. Well, here goes, I conjure the name of _____ to come forth and show himself to help me find some buried treasures! All I am interested right now is money! I want to be rich."

I waited a few minutes after it explained what I was to do, but I thought to myself that nothing even happened—how can that be! I know I would be scared half to death if something did appear. "How will I handle it if they do? Well, the book says they are friendly so I shouldn't have anything to worry about." I continued calling out three or four different names and reading the magic rite for these spirits to come forth. For about 15 minutes, I just listened. But nothing. "No scary stuff happened, nothing did! Hmm, I wonder if I had even done it right?" I just hoped some of these guys would know who it was that I was calling for because I was far from pronouncing some of their names properly. But I asked myself, "They should know I want them to come to my house here because of the other guys I called. I'm sure that I said their names right. If they are friends with each other at all, they would just go get their buddies, right?" As I continued reading the chapters, it said that there are good spirits and bad spirits. The good ones are caught in limbo and don't want to die for some reason, or maybe they are not at peace with death in order to leave this earth yet.

"The good ones are the ones I want, the ones that might be hanging around where I live in Standish. They might be able to show me where in the area the hidden treasures are. I just hope I don't get any of the bad spirits here, the book doesn't' say much about them. They must be the people that turned evil before they died, the book says, and there may be spirits that are just plain evil. I guess they would have to have some good inside of them if they are going to show me where all the hidden money is, right? They just can't be plain evil! Well, it's been about twenty minutes, so I guess this stuff isn't going to work. Maybe I did it wrong, or maybe I didn't read the book right! Well, I'll just have to put it up for a while and when I have more time to read, I'll do it again. I may have done something wrong in the ritual But for now, I'm just going to put it up on my TV and leave for Pete's Restaurant to see if anyone is hanging out."

A Few Days Had Passed

My mom called me a couple of days later. She was planning on moving back to Michigan to stay. She missed everyone and all the memories that went with the area. She didn't have any place to stay when she did come back, so I offered my place. One of my buddies decided to move back to his mom's house anyway, and that left me with one bedroom open.

About three weeks had gone by. My mom was all moved in and settled and we had just got back from having a family get-together. She hadn't seen everybody in a long time, so it was late when we came home. It was almost 11:00 p.m.. We were exhausted, so we went to bed.

Roughly 25 minutes had gone by, and I started to hear the dishes in the sink drainer clink back and forth. I also started to hear footsteps in the kitchen, coming towards the livingroom. They seemed to walk back and forth.

"Man, what in the world is that?" I asked myself. I tried going to sleep, and just reason away this sound that was so clear in the house. There wasn't any noise outside, no cars or people outside the window who could be walking down the sidewalk. I checked the windows and they were closed. I could only hear these footsteps walking around the living room and in and out of my bedroom. It was not coming from outside. The footsteps grew louder, and it began to bother me. "What in the world was that?" I asked myself, then more dishes began clicking together. I finally fell asleep after laying in bed after about an hour.

When I woke up the next morning, I had a short thought about last night. It soon went away—it had to be my imagination what happened. I didn't say anything to Mom. about it. I just went into the bathroom and reached for my toothbrush. After that, I combed my hair and left for work.

That Night

When I got back home, I didn't have to take the truck up north. I was home early that evening. As I walked in the door, I said "Hi," to Mom and sat at the kitchen table with her. She said to me: "I don't know what's going on in this house, but I kept hearing things off and on throughout the day. I left my cigarettes on the table, went to get a glass of water, and when I turned around my lighter was gone! I had just set it on the table next to my cigarettes. I don't know what's going on, Randy. The next thing I did was some cleaning in the living room. Then I was in the bathroom for a while, and when I came back out my lighter was back on the table next to my cigarettes!"

I just thought she was hallucinating or something myself. I didn't know what to say to her, so I just shook my head and gave her a dumbfounded look. We talked more while I helped mom do the dishes and put them in the dish drainer next to the sink. We watched TV for awhile.

I stayed up until about 11:30, then decided to go to bed. About 25 minutes had passed and the footsteps started. I heard the dishes clinking back and forth in the dish drainer, so I hollered out to Mom. I asked her, "Do you hear that noise?"

"Yes?" she replied in a very nervous tone, "What do you hear, Randy?" All of a sudden, I heard someone playing a piano or an electric organ of some kind, and some people were singing. I yelled, "Mom! Do hear that music?" She came running into the bedroom, and replied in a whisper, "I can hear it." I looked around in the corners to see if someone had left a radio, or maybe the alarm had turned on. I told Mom, "I'm not going to find a radio because I don't have one in the house."

These things happened night after night and it was scaring me, that's for sure. After a few nights, the footsteps came closer to my bedroom, and then next to my bed. Whatever it was, it started growling. It sounded just like an angry dog. I got up and looked around and could not see a thing—I even started laughing a little to myself. "What is going on with me? Am I going insane or crazy?" I fell asleep about two or three hours later, but I was tossing and turning most of the night, disturbed by the noise of whatever that thing was "growling." I was so frustrated, trying to figure out what had happened to cause this. Had I done something? Was there something wrong with this house that we don't know about? What could have started this, or evoked it? I wonder if that book will ever send me someone to find that treasure I wanted?

Over the next few days

The harassment increased day by day. "They" started crawling on the bed, and crawling on me, my pillow, scratching on the wall. There seemed to be about three of them, and they crawled between my legs. I could feel their heavy breath when they bit my legs. They didn't puncture the skin, but it was enough to get my attention. They chanted my name wickedly and repeatedly: "Randy, Randy," all night. If these were the spirits I summoned, they were not communicating—they just wanted to torment me.

This went on night after night. Weeks went by, but they did not tire. I wished I knew what it was they wanted from me. I would pause for a moment or two thinking and wondering: did I do this? Then, "I don't believe these are the good spirits. I must have called up something evil, maybe? But what do they want? What are their plans?" I tried to speak to them and asked questions several times, but there were no answers or comments from them, just constant harassment all night long. I talked with my mom about it one morning over coffee. She understood and had an open mind which was a huge relief. I spoke in private to some close personal friends I had chosen to confide in, but my story was very hard for them to accept.

Weeks Had Gone By

Fear began to grip me like never before. Depression started to set in deeper and deeper as the days turned in to weeks. I did everything I could do to hang in there and keep my sanity. During the day, quite often we could hear an organ playing in the house upstairs and two women singing or just talking. We were both too scared to go upstairs and check it out. After a while, it would just stop and we would forget about it. I would go outside and walk around the house to see if it was the neighbors. But nothing could be heard from outside. It would still be playing in the house when I returned. And one day, it became a real problem.

A case worker from the Social Services office came over to talk to Mom about my two sisters. She walked in that day, and after she introduced herself to Mom she sat down on the chair next to the bedroom. Suddenly, an electric organ started playing real loud from upstairs. It scared the tar out of my mom and I. We did not have any idea how to explain the organ noise if the case worker asked about it. After a few minutes had gone by, the case worker couldn't help but ask: "Who's the person playing the organ?" It was very loud and very annoying this time. Mom was very nervous, shaking inside and trying to hide what she was hearing. She avoided the question and kept talking about other things to try and get the woman's attention on other subjects. But to no avail, it didn't work. The case worker asked again, about ten minutes later: "Who is that person playing the organ? One of your children?"

"Oh boy, here we go," Mom said to herself. "No, I think Randy left the radio on upstairs," she replied in a shaky voice. Her hands were trembling also as she pointed to me. I just looked around the room and tried to pretend I didn't hear Mom say anything. I was in too much shock to answer myself. I just passed it off and it worked, because Mom got her on another subject! "What do you tell a person from the State Department?" I asked myself.

After about an hour went by, she finally was finished with her questions and she decided to leave. Mom and I were so relieved when she finally left that we just laughed for few minutes about how funny it was. But at the time, we were going through lot of frustration trying to deal with it. It wasn't funny then. "Oh God, what is happening in this house? What do we do?" asked Mom.

I headed over to Pete's Restaurant after we ate supper to see if anyone was around. I ran into some friends of mine drinking coffee. I made sure no one noticed anything different about me and I just acted normal. I didn't want anyone to see any fear or panic. I didn't want a situation where I had to explain my sanity.

"Hi guys. What's happening?" I asked them. Tim responded first.

"What's going on today?"

"Oh not much," I responded. Jerry asked me, "You're not working today?"

"No," I replied, "It's just a day of rest for me. But what are you guys up to?" So we just hung out for awhile and talked. Another friend of mine stopped in and sat down with us. It was quite a while before I did my other my errands.

Chapter Three

My Nightmare Deepens

One afternoon, I was sitting and watching TV while Mom was cooking up some supper. I began to hear something over top of the TV, like something was scratching behind door to the spare room that Dad used for storage. I walked over and put my ear to it and it was louder. "Wow," I thought to myself, "Mom!" I yelled, "there's something behind this door scratching. You should come over here and listen."

" Like what?" she replied, dumbfounded as she walked over and put her ear next to the door. Suddenly, something reached out, grabbed her by the throat and began choking her. She started crying and was gasping for air, trying to breathe while trying to get my attention. I was next to her, but I was frozen with terror—I really didn't know what to do.

"Mom! What's the matter?" With what little voice she could get out of her mouth, she cried out "Help me!" She was so scared, but she continued to struggle while trying to grasp at this thing that was around her throat, this thing I could not see! She cried out loud: "I can't breathe!"

"What are you trying to say, Mom?" I was frantic—I was struck dumb—I didn't know what to say, and my mind went completely blank! I was so full of fear, all I could think was: Mom is dying, what should I do? How do you fight something you cannot see? "What do I do?" I cried out to her. She pointed to a bible we had set out on the table since the haunting started. So I handed it to her and as she took it in her hands, suddenly it all stopped just as fast as it started. She ran in the kitchen and started sobbing uncontrollably. "What was that thing, Randy?"

"I don't know," I answered as I shrugged my shoulders in fear She turned off the cooking stove and said in a terrified voice, "We are leaving this house, right now!" We both hurried out the door and got into the car. We headed to my Aunt's house (my mom's sister) for some safety.

Well, as you might imagine, it was very hard to explain some things to her once we arrived. She only lived about seven miles from our house. After a while, Mom cooled down. She stopped crying and wasn't so scared anymore. After we explained what happened, my Aunt told us that we needed to get out of that house. She felt something very bad was going to happen in the near future if we didn't. She had many superstitious beliefs, and she explained that this was an "omen of warning" to us. "You have to get out of that house, and get out as soon as you can," she said. We didn't really have anywhere else to go just now, but she felt that we needed to get out at least before Halloween night, only four weeks away. We stayed with her for a couple of hours until Mom was feeling better about returning to the house. We returned to the house later that night and my Aunt gave us some instructions that she wanted us to carry out when we arrived.

I crept into the house and Mom stayed in the car until I checked things out. I was terrified, wondering what these things wanted from us. I thought they wanted their house back. So I proceeded with what my aunt had told me to do, and started reading some psalms from the bible on the coffee table. I went straight up to the closet. Boy, was I scared! My heart was pounding 100 miles an hour, so fast I thought it was going to climb right out of my throat. But a lot of peace came over me while I was reading, and I stayed at the door for at least five to ten minutes.

Whatever had been there was gone. Oh man, was I glad! I went to the car and coaxed Mom inside. When she finally stepped over the threshold, she was filled with fear and felt terrorized. She went straight to the kitchen as fast as she could.

I didn't hear the scratching anymore after that terrifying afternoon, and we never found out what caused it or why it was just in that room alone. My Dad kept it locked up and I didn't have a key to go inside. But it was one memory we tried soon to forget. Mom finally became peaceful after a couple of hours, but she made sure she never got close to that closet door again after that day.

After my Aunt's warning, we concluded that the spirits wanted their house back. Because of this mom and I had spent days looking in the Standish newspaper for another place for us to move into. It was not an easy task, but we made sure we went right to the newspaper office to get the newest release. We also asked around town and drove down every road we could find to see if any houses had a sign in the window at all about renting. We were not going to waste any time, and we were not going to stay any longer than we had to.

After a few days, I did get up the nerve to stop in at a Methodist church in the area. I stopped outside of the entrance and thought to myself, "Okay, how do I do this?" Well, I finally decided to go in—I really had no choice but to try. If the pastor here couldn't help me, there were a lot more churches beside this one. I was going to try every one of them if I had to. I opened the door and the secretary was in the office. I asked if I could meet the pastor for some conversation, and she said, "Wait a moment and let me see if he is free."

"Okay," I said to myself, "well, this is it. He's even here." She came back and said, "You can go in his office; it's right around the corner."

I walked and introduced myself "Hi, I am Randy." We both shook hands and he asked me, "What can I do for you, Randy?"

"Well," I said, "It's hard to explain my situation, but I'll see if I can." I spent about five or ten minutes telling him some background and he replied:

"Well, I don't know how to deal with a situation like this, Randy. I have never come across anything quite like your dilemma. I really don't know what kind of advice to give you, or where I could send you, even."

How depressing—a "house of God," and he doesn't know how to help someone who is being tormented by the Devil. He did comment that it could be the Devil though, yet he didn't have any knowledge on how to help. He thanked me for stopping by and wished me luck in finding someone who could help.

A friend of mine told me every church has different beliefs, and maybe I'd come across someone who could help if I just kept looking. From time to time I stopped when I saw a church on my route or was just passing by. But I received the same story in return: no one had an answer.

We found a trailer house to rent, northeast of Pinconning. It was about 55 feet long and about 16 feet wide with four bedrooms. One was an addition to the house, a very large place. It took us two days to move in, but it only took a few hours for these spirits to start their taunting again. I went to bed one night and began hearing the noises as I had in the other house. I got up and shut my door quickly, but what good did that do? If these things were spirits, they would just walk through the door. I still wanted it closed. At least that might keep one of these guys from showing up at the door suddenly. That would scare the pants off me. It was already enough that the noise was getting louder. They started their scratching on the walls again and chanted my name out loud: "Randy, Randy."

What was I to do? "Please, God, if you are alive, please help me!" I begged him almost every night. I was given a large wooden crucifix by a family friend. It was about two and a half feet in length. I kept the crucifix on my chest and left a bible open on my dresser each and every night.

Chapter Four

Was This An Answer To My Prayers?

Months Had Gone By

My mother had run into an old friend of the family while visiting in Detroit who asked how the rest of the family was doing. They talked for a long time, and Mom started to share a little bit about what I had been going through. She started crying while explaining it—she couldn't hold it back..

Sara, her friend, said, "I have a brother-in-law and I know he could help you."

"Oh, really?" Mom responded.

"Yes," Sara said, "He does work just like this at home."

"Like what?" Mom asked.

"He deals with the spirit world directly. He's a Witch, a White Witch." Sara said.

"Wow, that sounds pretty awesome. How can I get ahold of him?"

Later on that day, Mom filled me in on the conversation she had with her friend Sara. I had met Sara in the past a few times.

"Sara called her brother-in-law on the phone while I was down there, and he's coming up here this weekend," Mom said excitedly.

"Wow, that sounds awesome indeed! I hope he can bring this nightmare to an end," I replied anxiously. I was very happy inside as she continued to explain what he did and where he lived in Detroit.

It Was A Few Days Later

It was Friday already and we heard a knock at the door. I was sitting at the kitchen table, eating with Mom. I got up and answered the door. "It must be that guy, Mom," I said. I opened the door to let him in and he introduced himself.

"Hi, I'm Perry." I welcomed him in as he came through the door.

Just a few minutes before, my mom had put a pot of coffee on to brew. It was an old coffee pot that made a lot of noise, and we forgot about it having been plugged in. During Perry's introduction, it started to make the awful noise it always does when it's ready to be poured—*woo woo*, very loud. Then it would make a big *snap* and then *pop!* It would keep *woo woo*-ing until Mom picked it up to pour the coffee. Well, of course Perry was startled right out of his pants when he heard it. Mom and I just started laughing our heads off because we knew it was the coffee pot.

"Is that the ghost you guys have in the house?" Perry asked me.

"No," we replied, "It's the coffee pot."

"Wow," he replied as he laughed uncontrollably, "I thought it was already starting something with me."

Well, that sure broke the ice with everyone, and he began to explain what he did in his spare time besides working at a GM plant in the Detroit area. He said he was a White Witch under the headship and authority of the Wicca Church of Witchcraft in the Detroit area. He also held a college degree in (I believe) Natural Living. It all combined together with Witchcraft, he said. He had been a Priest in this discipline for about ten years.

My mother and I didn't have the faintest idea what witchcraft was, nor did we have any knowledge of the "world of the occult." As he finished talking about his trip up here, he started putting some of the equipment he brought with him on the table. He laid out some things he wanted me to wear: amulets and magical medallions, all the different names of God on them. I couldn't even pronounce the names. One had written on it *Tetragrammaton.* One was to protect me from the evil eye, and another was to protect against the evil spirits of black magic. He also gave me some bible scriptures on parchment paper to carry in my wallet. The amulets and medallions I had to wear around my neck at all times, he explained. In addition, I also had to wear a few different kinds of crosses.

Mom asked him if he would like to stay for a while, that he was welcome to do that instead of going back home on Sunday night. "I think you are going to be here for a while," Mom told him. He loved the idea. This way, he could spend a few days discerning the situation and get some background on everything. This would also give him sometime to come up with a plan, he explained to us. He also had a deck of tarot cards that would enable him to speak to the spirit world or read a person's future, but that wasn't all. He had many different tools of the occult with which to contact the spirit world in order to get answers or to just foretell the future, past or present. He actually had a side job searching for loved ones. He spent time praying for broken relationships to heal, he searched for lost animals, rings, etc..

He explained that he wasn't going to charge me because of the magnitude of the situation. It would be his gift to me for him just to be able to participate in bringing this nightmare to end and getting the experience he needed for his Ministry. He was definitely an answer to my prayers.

We didn't speak to each other much through the week to come. He was very busy for the next few days while gathering up information and some background to discern the situation. I often saw him in trances, reading tarot cards and trying to communicate with the spirit world to gather additional information he needed. When he did a personal reading for me, the cards did tell him that I had a curse on me somehow. But, he explained, he would talk to me later about it. He wanted to explain a little about himself first.

He told us that he was a good Witch, the "White" standing for good things, and that he always used the bible in his work. He wasn't into black witchcraft because it was the other side. It was used for evil purposes. He was not a person to bring harm to anyone. But if it was necessary, he would use it for self-defense purposes only—to stop anyone who would bring him or someone else harm, he further explained. Gray magic was just the balancing of the white and the black magic together to bring forth a good outcome. I was so impressed that he used the bible. That definitely gave me the confirmation I needed—he was an angel sent by God!

One morning, while we all were drinking our coffee at the kitchen table, Perry asked, "Do you guys think we could go up to the house you guys lived in before? I would like to take some oil and water with me. I'm going to bless the house—maybe I could do some kind of an exorcism in the house. Maybe try to drive these spirits back to where they came from?"

"Well," I told him, "yes, I think that could be arranged. We can go up right now after we finish our coffee if you want. How's that sound, Perry?" He replied, "That sounds great. I'll go and pack some things that I'll need to take with me." Well, we headed up there a little later, after Perry was ready. I thought to myself, "I swore I would never come back to this place once I left."

WWas There a History Behind
The House on Church Street?

The house was eerie-looking all by itself as we pulled up the driveway. It had a personality of its own. It felt like the house was waiting for you, as though someone was staring from the windows.

"I can feel the spirits that are here." Perry commented as soon as he went in the door. Man, I thought to myself, that guy sure is gifted with powers from God. The house was one hundred years old or more, and looked it. On the north side of the place, part of the foundation was sinking into the ground. This made it even more eerie-looking. It was a two-story house with old windows in the front, and a dark cloud-like cast hung over it. My dad had never re-modeled it or changed any of its appearance since he had purchased it.

"My friends were always afraid to come inside anymore after they found out what had happened." I explained to Perry as we walked in the front door. My dad kept a lot of antiques in the room from which my mom was attacked, and he had put some upstairs. Perry felt they may have had a curse on of them. He told us that sometimes the first owner would put a curse on them and then sell them to someone they hated.

"So that could be the reason your mother was attacked, Randy." When we went inside, the first thing, Perry did was open his bible. He began reading scriptures throughout the house, going from room to room while blessing the windows and the doors on his way into the next room. When he was done blessing the house and praying over it, he attempted to do an exorcism. He went back into every room and hung a "mojo bag" on each window. I asked what they were and he replied, "I have a mixture of different herbs and spices, the kind that evil spirits hate, and I am hoping it will drive them out of here over a period of time."

Suddenly, he started to hear voices from the spirits in the house. He tried to put his hands over his ears to block it out, but it didn't work. They screamed into his ears as though they were in pain from his blessing the house. They were screaming repeatedly, over and over, and in a voice that no one else in the room could hear, told him that he was not going to be allowed to set me free from them. They owned me. "He belongs to us." They continued to speak this into his ears until we left the house. He did not let it shake him, but it did startle him! He didn't share this warning with me until weeks later, thinking it would do more damage than good.

It did scare me when he decided to tell me. It put unspeakable fear into my heart. I can still remember that day he came in my bedroom and sat down next to me and began to explain to me what had happened. It was so awful, and so hard to believe! A depression came over me like never before as he continued to explain the best he could. I had thoughts of hopelessness: Will I ever get free from them? Is it true? Do they own me? Is this possible? Is Perry unable to help me after all? Oh God, please help me—where are you?

He explained before he left my room he wasn't going to give them any power by releasing any type of fear in himself, so he stayed strong for me and walked with a positive attitude when he left that house. "I wanted to keep this to myself," Perry said, "and I still think I can help you, Randy. I just need you to put your trust in me, and I'll keep trying. Or do you want me to stop?"

"No," I replied, "Please keep trying, okay?"

Perry said, "I definitely will keep searching for some more answers till I come up with a permanent solution." But he was unsure if what he had done in the house was going to work. Did it just agitate them some more and make them angry?

A Few Days Later

Perry approached me and explained he wanted to do a ritual that night. It would have to begin at 11:00 p.m.. There would be a full moon. So I waited around a while and read some of the books that he had. It was getting very close to 11:00 p.m. and Perry yelled out for me to come help. I went into the kitchen and, as he instructed, began laying out the masking tape in a large circle on the kitchen floor, about eight feet across. Before I laid the last piece of tape, we all had to get inside the circle. Only then could I close it. That would complete the circle and close any open doors that the enemy could use during the session, Perry explained. At each point of the magic circle he would place a white candle along with the name of the angel each candle represented, for protection. According to his log, the angels were coming on duty about 11:30 so he was going to summon them to help us at that time. Everything had to be in its place by that time. He then began placing all the different names of God at the different points of the circle. He found these names in the bible, he told us, names like Jehovah, Yaweh, Alpha and Omega, Tetragrammaton, Yod-He-Wa-Hee, and many others. Then he faced the east and laid out a white linen cloth on the table and placed two tall white candles in the middle. He then brought out a large, hardcovered book that was encased in pages and pages of parchment paper. It was a very powerful holy book of magic, rituals, and invocations, that only his eyes could look upon. It contained the procedures for certain kinds of rituals for calling up spirits from the spirit world and to communicate with them. These were rituals he had gathered over the years and personally had liked to work with the most. He had placed many scriptures in his own handwriting from the bible in each chapter. It held the power to force back or remove any evil that was coming against a person's life, and to take a life if needed. Next to it he placed a copy of the King James' Bible to look things up or use the power of the bible itself if needed. I tried to be as still as I could and to say as little as possible. The house was very quiet inside. No noise of anything was allowed. Around the table he put out bells, trinkets that made noise, candles, incense, different types of amulets, and several crosses.

"Well," Perry said, "I'm all prepared to talk to anyone that desires to show up to help us find some answers, Randy." The candles began flickering. When he saw them flickering, Perry explained to me that it meant that the angels he had summoned had arrived. Perry began to read from his holy book, and was seeking a vision. He went into a trance many times, read from his personal holy book, then read some scripture. Then he laid out the tarot cards to see what the cards had to say.

I was very nervous inside, wondering what was going to happen next. Mom was also looking around the room, watching for anything to move. We both were very scared, not even knowing what to expect at one of these sessions. It was a calm night outside and very quiet indoors. The light from the candles was the only thing that moved in the room. When they flickered across the walls and the furniture it created an atmosphere of eerie shadows as we waited patiently.

Three hours went by and nothing! Perry was getting very disappointed at getting no response from his attempt to communicate. Perry said, "I can't hold the angels here anymore. They must be released, their shift is up. I just can't seem to break through to the spirit world and contact anyone, so I'm going to take everything down and put all these things away. We need to do this another day when I can break through, okay, Randy?"

Well, I was tired and went to bed after helping Perry clean up. I was so depressed—why didn't God show up? Where is he, what's going on? I had been so excited and looking so forward to this and it turns out to be a dud. He tried to explain to me, to make me feel better, that in many cases he would be contacted at a later time after doing a session like this. I did find out later from Perry, about several days later actually, that something did happen that night.

He felt it triggered in the previous smaller sessions that he done a few days earlier in private.

The House Wasn't What They Wanted

Well, I know that night after I went to bed that something was "triggered," because after 20 minutes in my bedroom trying to get some sleep, things were beginning to start. But tonight it was all different. I began hearing a harp playing next to my bed, like a harp that would be played in heaven by an angel. In some way it gave me enough peace that I could stand the fear filling my heart. Yet I still heard growling. It was coming from more than just three of them this time—there were several more. Fear began to well up inside me.

They began terrorizing me. They continued to crawl on my bed and scratched on the walls, calling out my name repeatedly: "Randy, Randy, Randy." But this time it was more fearful than ever before. It sounded like they were coming down the hall to kill me. I was so full of hopelessness and dread—why didn't Perry's plan work? I never knew something this horrifying existed. It seemed to triple what I had been experiencing before. When was it going to end? "God, where are you?" I cried, in tears. I was so afraid of dying at the hands of whatever was after me. It was very late in the night when things calmed down enough that I could get at least a little sleep. I don't know how I even slept when I did. I guess exhaustion could be the only reason. I would wake up in the morning and everything from that night would be gone—but not my memory of what had happened.

Chapter Five

I was Drawn Deeper into the Supernatural

Two weeks later, Perry explained to me he wanted to do another session that night. There would be another full moon out, "and I need you, Randy, to stick around, okay?"

"Okay," I replied. So that night about 7:00 p.m. Perry dressed up so he could bless the house and the grounds and put up a protection barrier around us. He put on a thin, dark black gown that hung down to his shoes and a large pointed hat. They both had the many names of God printed on them in bright gold.

He took some water, poured it into a vase, put a little salt in it and blessed it with scripture before he went outside. He also took his bible with him and read scriptures while sprinkling water around the house trailer. He came in from outside a while later and went in went his bedroom and changed his clothes. When he came out later he brought a box for me full of candles of all different sizes, but very large ones. "These are for you, Randy," he explained, "You have to burn these candles one by one, twenty-four hours a day, and you must make sure that not even one of them goes out, or your protection barrier goes down. Each one will last at least four hours each." I thought to myself, "That will be a very difficult task since I have to drive truck during the day for work. How do I keep the candles from falling over in the truck?"

I helped Perry with taping the floor like last time. He kept all the things he needed in a box, the tools of his trade. He started placing them on the white linen sheet that he had laid out on the table. I continued to seal in the circle around us with the tape while he put out the names of the angels that we were to summon for protection. We turned out all the lights in the house. The kids were asleep in the bedroom, and we just had candlelight glowing in the room we were in. The setting was more eerie than the previous session we'd done. The wind had been blowing very hard outside all day; it didn't let up. I looked outside the window of our kitchen and it seemed to be blowing even harder than earlier. But maybe that was just my fear welling up in me or my imagination. It was very quiet inside the house, but the trailer itself was noisy. It creaked and moved from the wind pushing directly against it. The roof even made noise from one side to the other.

Perry's plan was to go a lot deeper tonight into the supernatural. It was a more powerful type of communication to contact the spirit world. Perry asked Mom to be in the circle with us, also under the protection. I didn't really know how to help him in any other way, so I just stood there and listened while he prayed from his personal Holy Book, in which he had prepared written information and directions he wanted to use just for tonight.

"Well," Perry replied after a few minutes, "I just broke through and I communicated with someone, and I am being told there's a curse on you, Randy. Now what I have to do is reverse it, and I'm going to carve an image from this potato and send it back to the person that was supposed to have sent it to you, Randy. I usually use a doll but I don't have one with me right now so I'm going to use this potato. It works the same way. Some call this 'Voodoo.' It's of the dark side of Black Witchcraft," he explained, but it was not to do any harm, just to return the curse back to its owner. He already had the image of a person cut out. He lit some incense that he had placed on the table earlier, and he began pushing pins through the potato as he prayed some kind of a ritual prayer from his personal book. I was watching in amazement and it all sounded right to me! "If someone is being evil and trying to harm me, then I want it sent back to them," I thought to myself. I watched him stick pin-like needles into the head and different places on the body as he prayed, facing the east.

When he was done, he laid it down on the table in front of him. Well, the winds seemed to blow harder and harder just at the same time and it caused a lot of rumbling on top of the trailer. It even sounded like someone was running up and down on the roof, from one end of the trailer to the other. "Did you hear that noise, Perry?" I asked "Yes," he replied. I just looked at Mom and she was pretty nervous herself. It may have had to do with what we were doing, but I wasn't sure myself. I really didn't know what to expect. It was just all very eerie—indeed, for all of us, even Perry! Just then, Perry gripped the table as he looked outside the window he was facing and said "Did you guys hear someone screaming?" "No," we replied. He had thought maybe someone was trying to get across the barrier he had put up around the house. Perry quickly went into a trance to try and communicate with whoever it was outside. But after a few minutes, he explained he wasn't able to communicate with whoever it was. After about three hours, Perry stopped praying and seeking more visions.

He decided to stop and release the angels, and started taking things down and putting them away. The wind also seemed to die down after a while throughout the session. It was so strong all day and night, was it just a coincidence? If I had let my imagination go and think this over, the wind that came in would have sounded like the forces of hell raising up and pounding against the trailer trying to fight Perry at what he was doing. My mom was thinking that also, but we didn't repeat it out loud. We were scared enough already by what was going on. I helped take up the tape and put some of his things in the box and got myself ready for bed. I thought to myself, "I wonder what I can expect tonight, relief or something worse?"

It wasn't too long before everything picked up where it left off the night before, another night of torment! There definitely was no change. I began to hear something from outside of my room just above my head where I had been lying down. All of a sudden, a loud roar came from some kind of huge beast outside my bedroom wall. It sounded like it was about eight feet tall. It seemed very huge in size if it were actually to be seen by the naked eye. I became so frightened I couldn't even move an inch, I was frozen in my bed. I thought for sure it was coming after me. "Oh God, where are you?" If these are all devils or demons, it only convinced me that there had to be a God somewhere who had created them. I was so convinced that what Perry had done tonight would end it all.

I just didn't understand—why? Why? What was wrong with my life? Why won't this horrible nightmare stop? God, where are you? Why can I not find you? I am convinced you exist, because there are demons after me! I pulled out the huge wooden crossI had been using night after night. It had the body of Jesus on it—it was a crucifix. I held onto it as if I were gripping life itself. I placed it on my chest and cried out to God all night long because so much fear, and terror was overcoming me. It was going to be a very long night.

Chapter Six

Confrontations with the Supernatural

I cried my eyes out through most of the night with the fear that they were coming in after me. I prayed and pleaded with God to please help me! When I woke up late in the morning, I just happened to look at the bible I had placed on my bed that last night. It looked like someone's fingernails had torn through the paper, with three marks all the way to the bottom of the page. I was amazed by it. Later that morning, I showed Perry. He was very shocked and dumbfounded. All he could do was shake his head in disgust at all the things I had explained that had happened. He sat down on his bed in total confusion over what was still happening with me. I just looked at him and asked myself, as he paused in our conversation, "I wondered if suicide would end all this?" I had a strong will to live and to fight. Yet my depression grew deeper and deeper, and hopelessness set in as the days turned into weeks.

The next morning I was sitting at the kitchen table drinking my coffee. My little sister Tammy, who was twelve years old at the time, and her friends who had stayed over the night before came out of the bedroom. I overheard them explaining to Mom what they had seen last night coming through their bedroom window. It scared her and her friend, they said. My mom asked if she could describe it, and she replied "Yes. It was about seven or eight feet tall and it had huge wings and big teeth, and it went down the hall to Randy's room. But I was too scared to move, Mom! We just stayed there and it came back in our room again later and went back out the window, so we just went to sleep because I was too scared."

I thought to myself, "Well, that probably explains what I heard last night through my bedroom wall." The fact that I was not the only one seeing these things, that these little kids were seeing them, meant I wasn't insane, right? Perry also overheard the conversation, so walked over and took a look at the picture the kids had drawn. He said, "It looks like Beelzebub, Satan's right hand man."

"What is going on, Perry?" I asked.

"I don't know, Randy, I don't know! I am going to see if I can find something that will tell me."

He went into the bedroom and got out some books he had and began searching. He had all kinds of stuff, every area of the occult one could find. He started placing all these books on the bed and going through them, looking for something. I've seen books on black magic, divination, Ouija boards, incantations, Voodoo, wooing (form of fortune telling—that's what it described on the cover of the book I was looking at), necromancy (speaking to the dead), charms and spells of all kinds (another book). Also, I Ching (another form of fortune telling), dream interpretation, using a pendulum (that's another form of fortune telling), pyramid power, another book on omens, one about karma, yoga, hypnosis, automatic handwriting analysis, reincarnation, numerology.

Perry sat down and talked with me in his bedroom for a few minutes and told me:

"You know, Randy, this is the biggest attack of the forces of evil I have ever come against in my life. I have never come against anything like this one. I didn't tell you either, Randy, I did something while I was in Detroit last weekend."

"What?" I asked him.

"I went to some of my parish priests and even my head priest, even some friends that have been in this for more years than I ever have. I explained to them what I have been doing to help you, and I asked if any one had any ideas. And not one person could inform me on what to do next. This weekend I going back home to do some things that need to be done and while I'm there, I am going to try and get ahold of my old school professor of witchcraft whom I studied under, and see if he has any answers, okay? So don't lose hope just yet, okay?" as he laughed.

It's hard to believe a year had gone by now. It seemed like forever to me, like time had stopped. I dreamed of the days when my smallest problem was worrying about how to make my car payment, or who I could borrow some money from to get some gas in my car. The little things in life we take advantage of, and forget the most important things. Like your health, a sound mind, peace of mind, liberty. I wondered what my future held. Would my life ever be normal again? How I hoped for that—please help me, Oh God, why don't you answer my prayers? Don't you care about me? Just please, tell me what you want me to do, and I'll do it.

My friends came over a few days later one night. Tim, Terry, Jerry, and I were all sitting in the living room, goofing around talking. Mom took my sisters and went shopping. Tim started to light up some joints and passed them around. Everybody was feeling pretty good about 30 minutes later.

We had some music playing, and this huge beast—maybe Beelzebub?—came up around the of the corner of the living room just then. But you could not see anything from inside the house. It gave a loud roar through the wall while we were all sitting there! It sounded like a huge Kodiak bear standing up on it's rear feet right next to the wall of the trailer. If a person was to measure the size from the ground up to where I heard it, it would have had to be at least nine feet tall. All the guys froze in their shoes.

Tim, who was a very deep believer in the Jehovah's Witnesses teachings just froze in his chair and couldn't move either. Jerry was sitting next to him and softly said, "What the heck was that?" with complete fear on his face. Tim just shook his head, he didn't know. No one could say anything for at least five minutes. We all waited to see if that was the end of it, or just the beginning of it. No one wanted to go outside and check it out, either. There was no argument with that, the terrifying nature of this beast was enough to keep us in the house for quite a while that night before anyone would leave.

Me, I was scared out of my pants, but I couldn't move from my chair either for about a minute or two. I thought it was coming for me, and that it was all over. But after a few minutes I got a grip on myself and nothing else happened. It was a one time thing. I don't know what prompted that beast to do this but it looked like it was gone. I began to realize that now my friends knew what I have been going through all this time.

A Few Days Went By

Well, a few days later Bill came over and asked if I wanted to move in with him, Jerry, and Tim. All of us could have a great time and just party.

"My wife just left me," Bill explained, "and I have the house all to myself. She will never be back, so what do you say?"

Well, it sure sounded like fun. "Okay," I replied, "I'll let you know, Bill, okay? What happens if she comes back later, and then we all have to find a new place to live?"

"I am not taking her back, I have wanted a divorce for a long time because I can't stand being married to her anymore, so there's nothing to worry about."

I gave into the idea and moved in a couple days later. I needed a change. I took everything I could get in my new bedroom over to his house. It was an old house, but it was nice inside I got to pick one of the bedrooms downstairs, next to the living room. We all chipped in to pay for the rent and it made it a lot easier. It was located in the town of Pinconning, right within the city limits. When Perry came back from Detroit, about two weeks later, I asked him over to a party we were having. The guys asked if he wanted to take the bedroom upstairs that was open and move in with us. He said "Yes, it sounds great. I'm not due back to work for at least another three or four months at GM."

"How come?" we asked.

"It's changeover time for the new models to come out for next year, so vacation time!"

Well, everybody got along just fine and we sometimes had party after party—almost every night.

Everyone liked Perry. He was very easy to get along with, he also smoked pot and did other things with us when we had a party. So he was adopted just about by everybody he met, even the girls at Pete's Restaurant. We all often hung out together, pretty much everywhere we went, and Perry would drop everything and just come along with us if he heard there was a party or just the gang hanging out.

It wasn't long before those same spirits moved themselves in to my new place. They sought me out no matter where I went. Nothing seemed to change their minds or defer their aggression.

One morning when I woke up, I was sitting in the living room and Perry come down from upstairs and began to talk to me.

"When I was in Detroit, I tried a few things and wondered if there had been any change."

"No," I replied, "no, not a thing, Perry." as I took a deep breath in a state of frustration and depression. I then shook my head. "Everything is pretty much the same."

"I have some friends coming to visit and to discern some things when they arrive."

"When?" I asked.

"Tomorrow."

We were sitting in the living room that night, Perry and I , when he went upstairs and came back down with this root-like thing at the end of a thick string, about a foot or so long at the end. I asked, "What is that?"

"This is a pendulum. It's a kind of a divination tool; you can ask it questions and it will answer your questions Yes or No."

"Wow," I thought, "that sounds very cool indeed. Let's try something, then." Perry asked the first question.

"Does Randy have a curse on him?"

It started to swing all by itself with no one moving it. I watched in amazement at how this thing worked. Perry said one swing to the left is "yes" and one swing to the right is "no." It swung to the left first for my first question. That was what Perry had wanted to hear to confirm some more of his convictions. I asked it a question next.

"Is there another place that holds the secrets to answers we need for this curse?"

It said yes. That struck amazement into both Perry and I. Perry quickly asked it another question.

"Is this the house on State Road I have seen that was part of Randy's family homestead property?"

It started to swing left first, very hard just then. "Wow," we both commented on that one. "What we need to do, Randy, is some night take some time and go out to this house for a visit." Perry asked another question.

"Where is this evidence located in the house—first floor? It swung to the right first, which means no. Perry made a comment to me. "I wonder if there is a basement in the house? I'll ask it—Is the evidence in the basement of the house?"

It swung to the left first.

"Well, there's our answer, Randy. We definitely need to check this place out."

"Why don't we go tonight?" I asked Perry.

"That sounds like a very good idea. Let's move on this as quick as we can."

It got dark quickly during the fall season. We left just after we ate supper, Perry and I. It wasn't too far a drive, about five miles maybe, to the house off the main roads. We got there and drove very slow by it to see if anyone was living in it and was at home. We then pulled into a farm-field driveway and parked our car. We looked to see if any cars were coming down the road before we headed for the house. There was a full moon that night—boy, was it bright. Perry whispered to me in a low voice. "Hey! Let's go through the ditch. It looks like it's very dry. I don't see any water in it, and there is a car coming down the road—hurry up!"

I ran down into the ditch with him, and we crouched down behind the weeds and willows that were growing very high. "Stop," Perry said, and we watched the car go by. We then started for the house again, walking slowly so no one would see us if they were inside the place. We stopped about fifty feet from the house and we could see pretty good. Perry said:

"Someone needs to go up to the house and look for the basement." I was too scared myself to do it, so Perry volunteered. I stayed in the ditch while he crept up, staying low in the weeds so he wouldn't be seen if someone was inside. It took him about five minutes, and he came back to where I was sitting on the ground.

"Randy! I'm over here! Wow, you are not going to believe what I found!"

"What?" I asked.

"I found the basement! I started down the steps and I was stopped by a pool of blood!"

"What?" I said, with a shocked look on my face.

"It was definitely blood, Randy, because I used my flashlight to look it over and I touched it with my finger. It looked like chicken blood too."

"So what does that mean?" I asked Perry.

"Chicken blood is a sign of a curse. Someone does not want anyone coming into the house, so they applied chicken blood at the least-protected entrance of the house."

We sat there for a few minutes, thinking of what to do next. A truck was coming up the road, so we ducked down in the weeds of the ditch. Suddenly, the truck lost control and went down into the ditch! The driver started driving towards us as though it was manned by an evil spirit. Perry and I were terrified and started running towards the house for our lives, as fast as we could. The driver soon got control of the truck and pulled back out of the ditch with his four-wheel-drive on to the road again. He took off like someone was chasing him.

"What just happened, Perry?" I asked with fear showing all over my face. I was so dumbfounded and amazed after just being terrorized by something that looked like a clipping taken out of a murder mystery.

"Wow," Perry replied, "I don't know what just happened, I don't understand it but it sure looked like he was coming right for us, didn't it?"

Two minutes later, another car came by and it looked like the driver was having a hard time keeping his car under control. Perry said, "I think we better get out of here, now!"

"Yes," I answered, "let's get out of here."

So while we had the chance, we saw no more cars coming. We ran as fast as we could to the car. We jumped in and backed out and drove back to home. We talked a long time after we got home, trying to figure what was going on and why. The only conclusion we came to is someone or something, didn't want us around that property!

The Next Day

Well, Perry's friends were due up at any time. One of them was supposed to be a practicing Warlock, and the other was an experienced Sorcerer. Maybe it would help some to have somebody on the outside looking in, to maybe see things different.

Tim just came outside and sat next to me as I was staring off into nowhere.

"Good morning, Tim." I said.

"Oh boy, did I have a night," he said, "and I am still tired. What are you doing out here?" he asked.

"Just thinking about stuff."

"Like what?" Tim asked.

"I just remembered the card readings Perry did last night. Everybody was taking turns getting theirs read. When he came to mine—did you hear it, Tim?"

"No, what was it?"

"The cards said I was an evil person in the many past lives that I lived centuries before, and now I am paying for it with this torment. I didn't really believe too much in the Reincarnation theory myself," I explained to Tim, as I laughed, "I have a hard time believing that when a person dies he can come back as cow, or keep being re-born over and over till he gets it right."

Tim just shook his head and replied, "I don't know myself if there is such a thing, either."

Just then a car pulled into the driveway—Perry's friends from Detroit. Perry came outside just then and welcomed them all in. They already had a hotel room they were going to stay in for the night. We all visited for a long time that night, and they asked if they could go and see the house where it all started. Perry and I replied that we thought it would be just fine. The house was still empty; my Dad hadn't rented it out yet and I knew where the key was, so we got in the car and went up the house.

Chapter Seven

Desperation Drew Me Deeper Into Black Magic

Just before we arrived, Perry asked his friends if they could pick up the evil presence before approaching the house, without us telling them which one it was. I was very surprised at the gift of discernment they possessed. They pointed right at the house, and I was very impressed.

Well, we pulled in front, I got the key to the front door and we all went inside. They were very convinced that there was an evil presence, but they didn't have any ideas for us just yet. They said they would have to think it over and let Perry know, maybe tomorrow.

A Few Days Went By

Perry and I talked and that morning over coffee he shared with me that his friends still didn't have any more ideas than I had. Perry told me he had one other idea, but he wasn't sure if it would help my situation or not.

But, he went on to explain, there was an awesome book he came across in an occult bookstore he visited for the first time in Detroit.

"What is it about?" I asked.

"Well," Perry said, "there are only six copies in the whole world, and the store owner wants $125 for it," he laughed, "that's a lot of money. But," he went on, "I have been thinking about it for quite a few days and I think I'm going to stop by the store and buy it. I really want it now. When I go back home, I'm going down there next week, by the way—I have to pick up my check and do some things down there—and I'll stop by that store. I hope he still has it there and somebody didn't buy it already. I should be back in a couple of days."

I just sat there for a while and thought about things. I knew I was coming to the end of myself, and I was probably coming to the end of my life. I wasn't at all getting any encouragement from any of the ideas Perry had anymore. I would just answer him: "Let's give it a try, and see what happens." My faith in Perry and Witchcraft was dropping fast. Even though he had became such a good friend and had spent all his personal money on this venture, I could not see one event at all that he has tried that has really worked. Not even a small one. I was becoming convinced day by day that this was not the answer. But what was the answer? Should I try another church somewhere? Who's going to listen to this crazy story and actually believe me?

Perry was getting his things ready to head down to Detroit. Before heading out the door he commented, "I don't know if I'll have any time to read that book down there. But I'll have all week to check it out when I get back here, and I'll let you know if I find anything interesting. Okay, Randy?"

"Sure,"I replied, "I will be here. There is no place for me to go, Perry."

I was at the end of my road. I thought to myself, "I have been dealing with this nightmare now for about two years. Perry has even tried many seances to contact my deceased grandmother or anyone in the family that has passed on. But no one can get through the lines for some reason or another. Whatever Perry finds in this book I want him to do it, no matter what the cost. This is my last resort."

While Perry was gone I tried a few things on my own. I tried calling a lady in a newspaper I was reading who claimed she had powers from God. The ad stated that she could tell your fortune, bless your money situation, and remove evil spirits from you life. Now, that sounded very interesting but I wondered what was really involved. I called her up on the phone that day.

She answered after the second ring. "Hi, can I help you?"

"Yes, my name is Randy," and I went on to tell her my story. When I finished, she said that would be easy for her to do—all it would cost me was $450 for her services. What a rip-off, I thought to myself. So I asked her: "So if I send you the money, you can do this all the way from where you live in North Carolina? And what if it didn't work? Then what?"

"You would need to call me back," she explained. I replied, "Why are you using God's gifts to help people but charging money for it?" She tried to explain that was what she does, that if you want something then she charges for it. "If I had the money, you wouldn't get it from me anyway. Good-bye." I retorted.

I was so depressed after that conversation—how can a person who claims to be gifted by God charge you for her services? What about the poor and the needy who can not afford to pay for their freedom? I have always thought the gospel was free.

A Week Later

Perry pulled in the driveway the same time I did. I had just gotten back from my work.

"What's up?" I asked, all smiles as usual.

"Well, I got some good news. I bought that book—he still had the one copy left. He had to use a ladder to climb way up to the shelf were he hid it out of people's reach. I just took a short look and it's very powerful, it makes me shake all over. There's some very dark things in here. I'll look it over and see what I can find and I'll let you know, Randy."

A few days later, he told me he wanted to go up to Sara's house (she would be his sister-in-law, the one who introduced him to my mom in the beginning)

"Sure," I replied, "Let's go." He brought his tools of the trade, a box of things that he needed, with him.

Perry explained to me on the way up to the house that whenever he read this book he gets very sick and a horrible fear comes over him. He didn't know why. He could only read it for about 30 minutes at a time and would then have to put it down as this presence overwhelms him so much. Also, he explained that the book was written back in the 1800s and it had some of the first rituals and incantations ever written, the most powerful black magic and sorcery there was available—the darkest he had ever seen. "If this doesn't end everything, Randy, nothing will, because there is nothing left in the world of Witchcraft to use." He was simply amazed by this book. Perry then asked me:

"Randy? Are you ready for what I need to do? What is it you want to do? Well, I am convinced you have a curse still on you, and what the book has stated is that we have to reverse this thing properly. We do know that this person that put this curse on you is not backing off—that we know for sure. So the only conclusion I have left is the person has to be—well, how do I say this nicely?—this person has to be taken out of the picture, removed! Are you sure this is something you want to do, Randy?"

"Wow," I thought to myself for a while, just sitting in the car, "I have never harmed anyone in my whole life. How can I kill someone? I don't know if I can picture someone dying by my hands. But why is this person so angry at me that they want to take my life? Because that's what they are doing!" I told Perry my thoughts out loud just then: "So all I am doing actually is defending myself against this person, whoever it is. I wish I knew who it was."

Finally I answered Perry as we pulled up to Sara and Tim's house. He stopped in the driveway for a minute, waiting for me to finish talking.

"Well, Perry, I want you to do it because I want my life back. And whoever this person is, I want them stopped. If I have to take that person's life to get mine back, then let's just go in and do it, Perry."

So we went inside and visited for a while. Perry asked Sara if he could do this in her house where it would be more private than at our place. She quickly agreed and said sure, why not.

"Randy," Perry said, "I forgot to tell you something. When I was down in Detroit, I went over to the Church of Satan and asked if they please could help in any way. That's being hard up, let me tell you, Randy," as he laughed about it.

"So what did they say, Perry?"

"Well, they actually said they would only help if you and I would join their church and become members. I told them 'no, I don't want to do that. I will not join up with Satan to get him to stop.' So I told them thanks anyway, I'll find my own way."

So Perry got out all his stuff and started putting up his magic circle and placing the equipment around it. I asked if he needed any help, or if he needed us to do anything and he said no.

"Do I need to be in this circle, Perry?" I asked.

"No," he replied, "because this is going to be a different ritual from all the other ones. From what I understand, Randy, it's the most powerful Black Mass that's in the book, so I decided to use this one." Tim, Sara, and I just sat at the kitchen table drinking coffee and smoking our cigarettes as he went through his equipment and put everything in order on a table in the other corner of the dining room. He was using black candles this time, not the white ones. It made me think a lot while he was setting up. He had also dressed himself up in black while he was in the bathroom. I watched him pull out a real doll this time—not a potato.

Perry explained to us as he set up his things that if we all agreed, he would prepare a baptism for the three of us into witchcraft sometime if we wanted, and we could start our own Coven. It would include a new name for each one of us, and only the four of us would know them. Then we would greet each other after that with "Peace be unto," and "Brother" is where you would put your secret name.

"This is how one witch introduces himself to another witch in public. Another way to recognize another fellow witch is that we always wear a witch's claw around our neck or as a belt clip. I could do this in a couple of weeks, if you guys want?"

Tim and Sara thought it would be a great idea, but I had a lot of reservations myself. I really don't know if I want to be an actual White Witch or not.

Perry asked me for the last time before he started the Black Mass: "Randy, do you want me to still do this? I can still cancel this before I start."

"I have already thought it over enough so go ahead, Perry." I replied.

"Okay." He started to light the black candles and he got out his personal book of Holy Incantations and started reading. We just talked at the table between the three of us, and every chance I got I would look up to see what he was doing next. After about an hour, Perry received a vision from the spirit world. He spoke out loud for the first time in that hour.

"Well, Randy, I believe this is the right thing to do because of the vision I just got. I saw a cross with a pretty turquoise-blue background, and that color stands for the Holy presence of God! And as I put the pins in the doll, I could see someone screaming. I still couldn't tell who it was, though. That's still hidden from us."

I happened to look up at the cupboard next to Perry just then, and I saw one of the black candles melting into the shape of a cross. I yelled to him, "Perry, look up there—a cross!" He was overjoyed to see the confirmation he needed. It was another answer to his prayers. It also made me feel much better about what he was doing, so Perry continued to finish the Mass.

I watched Perry as he continued. He would read from his book and hold the doll up towards the west window while repeating some words and putting pins through the head and different parts of the doll's body. About an hour later he was finished and he began to pack his things away in his box. I really didn't feel any change just yet—I needed to be patient and wait for things to manifest in time.

We all sat down at the table. Perry said, "Boy, I could use a fresh cup of coffee, Sara," as he laughed. We just talked and laughed together through the rest of the night till about 2:00 a.m.. We talked about making plans for the baptism to be initiated as White Witches, but I was still hesitant. I just didn't know if that was what I wanted to be. Perry was kind of disappointed, but I told him I did not know yet whether I wanted to. I also had a problem with the ceremony, because everyone had to be totally naked in a circle. Then Perry would do a ritual and go to each person and kiss their groin area. All these things just grossed me out, plus it was winter-time almost and we would have to go out in the woodshed to do this. I just needed more time for that kind of a move in my life I told him, "I just can't do it right now, Perry, okay?" He nodded. "Yes, I understand." he said, and we talked about other things.

Months Had Gone By

Since I talked to Perry that night at Sara's when he had performed the Black Mass, the only thing I was sure of was that since Perry had come into my life and used Witchcraft, my life had gone downhill. Not one thing turned around for the better. I had even stopped smoking marijuana and cigarettes, I stopped drinking and taking all kinds substances, I didn't go to parties that introduced these. My depression had increased, I had lost my appetite to eat. I weighed about 90 pounds. My cheeks sagged in and the skin under my eyes had turned dark . I lost all hope and I was now living in hopelessness. I had no vision for the future. All I could think about now is that I just wanted to die.

Over the next few months, Perry came up for a visit one last time to his sister in-law's house. I came up also and we visited for while. Well, I asked if he would talk to me in private, and he said sure. We stepped outside on the porch while he lit up a cigarette.

"What's up, Randy?"

"Well, I would like you to do something when you get back home."

"Okay," he replied.

"I want you to stop everything you have done for me in the last few years, everything! I want everything reversed and all rituals, incantations, curses, everything you evoked disabled."

"Wow," Perry said.

"Ever since you began all this stuff, nothing has changed, stopped, or even gotten better—nothing! Alright, Perry? I really feel it has gotten worse actually. I'm sorry if I have offended you, Perry, but I am not trying to do that, okay?"

"Sure I can do that, Randy, and I will as soon as I return." Perry replied. I explained I wasn't upset with him because he had been a friend for so long and I knew he had tried his best to help me. I just needed to do something different. I needed to somehow separate myself from all this, to get my head cleared up and to try and see if I could find another way out of this mess.

Chapter Eight

God has Sent an Angel

I spent several months just seeking other churches, one by one. I found no help. No one had any answers, no one had any clue about what to do or where to send me. I asked myself: "Why is God not in these churches? Where is He? Why can't I find Him?"

A couple churches wanted me to check into an asylum for the insane! I could not find anyone who had ever dealt with something so dramatic, as my personal encounter with the supernatural. I even stopped searching for famous (or infamous) psychics. They listened but didn't help. They tell half-truths, mixed with soothing words that don't come to pass. I stopped all my seeking and started listening for God's voice, because I was on the verge of suicide.

I had no joy, no happiness, no future, no vision, nor any plans to live a normal life, but dying scared me—especially taking my own life. I still had, after all this time, a stubborn will to live, so I hung in there another few months. A year and half went by. All of us guys had moved out of the house where we had all been living in town. We went our separate ways, one by one, including Perry. He got called back to work at GM. After that, I only saw him that one day up at Sara's. I moved in with a friend of mine not too far away, just outside of town in a trailer across from Pete's Restaurant. I had lost all desire for partying, smoking and drinking. I stopped everything. The guys asked me to go out, many times but I turned them down. Over the many months, I experienced some changes in the nighttime harassments. Some of it eased up a little, and some didn't. Some nights were not full of terror but others still were. But still, I had no freedom, I still had lots of depression and oppression, and I was so empty inside but so full of hopelessness that the hole inside of me felt like it was a mile wide and ten miles deep.

Six Months Had Passed

One night, I ran into a good friend of the family whom I had not seen in couple of weeks (my cousin, actually) at Pete's Restaurant. We were sitting at a table on opposite sides of the room. When I saw her, I got up and took my coffee with me and sat down at her table.

"Hi, what's going on tonight, Cindy?"

"I am supposed to meet a friend up here for supper. I'm just waiting for her. So what are you doing, Randy?"

"Just hanging out," I replied.

She asked me what was wrong and I replied "What do you mean, what's wrong?"

"I know there's got to be something wrong with you because I can pick up depression immediately," Cindy explained.

"I'm amazed at you being able to pick up something like this, because you are right on the money, Cindy! How did you know?"

"I have felt it for a long, long time around you. I didn't know how to ask you."

"What else do you see?"

"Oppression and hopelessness, a lot of heaviness."

"Wow...well," as I hesitated, "I'm dealing with some junk and I can't find anyone to help me deal with it."

"What kind of junk?" Cindy asked.

"Well," I hesitated again, "I have some spirits after me, and they won't go away." I thought to myself, I can't tell her the whole story. She will think I'm a nut.

She immediately told me that her mother dealt with situations just like this.

"No way," I replied, "Right here in Pinconning? I have been looking all over the face of the earth for someone." I said to myself.

Cindy said, "I'll talk to her for you, if you want, and let her know you want to see her.

"Yes," I replied, "do that."

We also talked about riding together tomorrow to the unemployment office together. Our appointments were only a few minutes apart. I thought to myself, as I walked back to my table with my coffee, it was so difficult to find any faith in anything else, since I spent so much time and effort with Perry, who had tried everything he did to find answers, let alone freedom. I had to reach down very, very deep to even give it one more chance. One more person—I have told my story over and over throughout the years. It has been so exhausting!

Well, Cindy met me at Pete's the next day and we headed up to West Branch to the unemployment office. I brought up the subject up with her again about her Mom. She began to explain that her Mom belonged to the Catholic Charismatic Renewal. She would pray for people and awesome things would happen.

"So what does a Charismatic Renewal mean?" I asked her.

"It's a group of people in the Catholic Church who join together and play gospel music, sing, and worship God in the power of the Holy Spirit and Randy, awesome things happen! There are healings taking place and people getting set free from demons! This group of people are born-again and filled with the Holy Spirit."

This was a lot to think about all day. It sounded very interesting to me. We got our checks and headed home. Cindy dropped me off at my car which I had left parked at Pete's Restaurant. I told her I would call later that night.

Later On That Evening

The day went by fast. It was getting very close to about 7:00 p.m. already. So I called her but couldn't get through the phone line for about an hour. I must have dialed it wrong. So I changed the numbers around and I finally got hold of her.

Cindy answered and we talked for a little bit, and she said her mom wanted to see me that night. So I headed over to her house. It was only about two miles from where I was living at the time. I was in deep thought all the way over to her house. "What is this woman going to do? She's probably just a good talker and gives a lot of advice that doesn't go anywhere."

I knocked at the door of her hair salon, and her mom introduced herself. "Hi, I'm Judy."

"Hi," I replied. She asked me to sit down. She then pulled up a chair and started talking to me. I picked up a presence emanating from her that was so peaceful, I felt like I knew her all my life. She was a very loving person and easy to talk with. She didn't appear to have any special kind of power.

She was a very small person, about five feet tall and very thin. "How's this women going to do anything for me?" I asked myself. "She is so short, and such a small person. This woman casts out demons?"

"So, Cindy says you have a problem, Randy, that you need help with," she said to me.

"Yes," I replied, "I do."

"So tell me about it, Randy."

"It's not that easy to explain," I responded.

"That's okay," she replied, "just start at the beginning. I have got time!"

Well, I started to explain to her that I had this problem for at least three years or more, and that some evil spirits will not stop tormenting me. I could not find anyone to help me stop them. I just didn't want to live anymore. I couldn't find relief anywhere or from anyone. I continued to explain to her the whole ordeal, and I was so surprised at how receptive she was. She believed everything I said. She was not judgmental and listened to everything.

"So how did all this begin, Randy?"

"Well," as I paused to look back, "I think it started when I bought a book on witchcraft. I'm not sure, though."

"What did you do with the book? Did you read it, Randy?" she asked.

"I tried to call some spirits up to talk to me."

"That's how it all started, then, Randy. You opened some doors with this book." she explained. She responded with so much confidence and experience.

I had never had anyone talk with me like this before. I was so amazed by her response to my story. I kept feeling this presence that was around me, an awesome peace engulfing this huge empty hole inside of me. I felt so loved by someone and I didn't understand where it was coming from. All the fear I'd had for years was leaving me.

My depression began to leave as she introduced this Jesus person to me. I didn't really know who He was at that time in my life. She explained to me that witchcraft was wrong to get involved with, that it was very dangerous. That I opened the doors to the spirit world right then and there the moment I read that book aloud. She stated that the bible warns of the dangers of witchcraft and the occult. She explained further about the curses that come upon a person's life who gets involved with witchcraft.

"We have to close those doors, Randy. Jesus can set you free from all this nightmare, Randy!" she continued to explain who He was and how much He loved me and cared about me, and how this was not His plan for my life.

I explained to her that I was at the end of my rope and I just want to die if she couldn't stop this torment. She replied:

"Oh, but He can, Randy, He can stop this and that's what we are going to do tonight! Randy, I'm not letting you live another night like this again."

I thought to myself while she continued to talk. She had such conviction that this would be my last night of torment. I began to fill up with hope. I felt faith filling my being like never before. But I still had a problem with one question. I was asking myself: Why does this person want to help me? I'm a nobody! I'm not an important person! Why does He want to bother with saving me from all this suffering?

"What other kinds of things were you involved in, Randy? Randy?"

"Yes, sorry, I was thinking very deep, Judy." I continued to explain to her all of the occult areas and how I had asked Perry, a White Witch, to come up and help me out. I told her how he spent a few years up here with me and stayed with us. He practiced his magic to try and help me. She began to read a scripture from the bible that goes as follows:

> Jesus said, "I am the way
> the truth and the life, and
> no man comes to the Father
> but by Me.
> (John 14:6)

Everything she was saying to me was convincing me of the Truth. I was overflowing by then with more peace and I felt a supernatural presence. I had never felt this before. My whole being was filling up and it increased by the minute. It was so wonderful—my mind had been so full of confusion and so much fear, depression, and terror all this time. I felt this life-giving presence filling this place inside of me that had been so dead for so long. "Oh God," I thought, "what is this I'm feeling?"

"Now Randy," she said, "I want you to say a prayer, and I want you to repeat it out loud to me, okay?" She also explained it had to be from my heart, with meaning, and not to just recite it back to her. "Okay." I said.

Chapter Nine

You Shall Know The Truth And

The Truth Shall Make You Free

"Okay, repeat after me," she said:

"Lord Jesus Christ, I believe You died on the cross for my sins and rose again from the dead. You bought me with Your blood and I am Yours. I want to live for You, I am sorry for all my sins, known and unknown. I confess and renounce all of them. I now forgive everybody as I want You to forgive me. Forgive me now and wash me clean with Your blood. I am thankful for that precious blood of Jesus which cleanses me now from all sin. I come to You now for my deliverance. You know my needs, You know what it is that holds me captive, that torments, that defiles. That evil spirit, and that unclean spirit, I claim the promises found in Your Word. That, whosoever that calleth on the name of the Lord shall be delivered, and I call on You now. Satan, I renounce you and all of your works, I renounce all my involvement in the occult, and the witchcraft I was in. In the name of Jesus Christ, I command you Satan and all your kingdom to remove yourself from my life now..."

Judy started the deliverance, and when she looked up the whites of my eyes had turned black. She had a Christian radio station on also, which was playing music that ministered to me the whole time. She ask me to renounce the spirit of witchcraft out loud as she came against its hold on my life. Suddenly, something took hold of my mouth and my body. I had a very difficult time getting one word out at a time. When I was able to repeat it, I passed out and my body began shaking violently.

Something took my arm and began smashing and throwing the things she had on the counter for her hair salon. I then kicked my feet hard against one of the walls and I pushed one foot through it. I then started yelling and shoving the chair I was sitting in, it had wheels on the legs, it was one she used for her customers. I drove the chair all the way across the room from one side to the other by smashing my feet against the walls of her room. Judy continued to repeat her demands to the spirit of witchcraft:

"In the name of Jesus Christ, you loose Randy now, and leave him unharmed!"

I came to, and seeing what I had done to her room, I tried to explain to her that I could see something take control of my body and I could not stop him. There was also a clock across the room. It was in front of our view, and I noticed the clock jumped an whole hour while I was out cold. I could not account for any of that lost time. I told her how sorry I was for breaking those things in her room. She replied, "That's not anything to worry about right now. What's important is you getting set free. Now just relax," she continued. I tried, but I passed out again. From the back of my head, I saw and heard someone using my voice and yelling at her. There were horrible things being said to her through me. This evil spirit took full control of my mouth and my vocal cords and began swearing at her and calling her names. He told her she didn't know what she was doing, she was a nobody, and that she didn't have the faith to make him leave. He continued to laugh at her wickedly and say: "I will never go! And you can't make me!" She just shot back with, "I know who I am in Christ, and it isn't I who casts you out, but I cast you out in the name of Jesus Christ, and you are going to go!" Of course, this brought him pain and agony listening to that, and he jolted me up and down on the floor even more. After another 25 minutes had passed, the spirit of witchcraft did come out. He also took some smaller evil spirits that were under his command with him and left.

Judy continued to pray against the other demons that came to the surface and announced themselves pridefully and arrogantly. Some had to be forced to the surface that were hiding, and others just left quickly because they feared the presence of God. She knew most of the time who they were, because she was led by the spirit of the living God. The devil had picked the wrong person to mess with—a little hick-town woman, just five foot small, but fifty foot tall in her beliefs and her faith. She was not one to be moved or to be shaken! She refused to budge one inch from what she believed in! The Powers of Hell were leaving this man's life.

I woke up from time to time throughout this ordeal and the clock was facing me. It became the first thing I would see each time I opened my eyes. I watched one hour or more disappear. Many times I overheard different demons screaming in pain when Judy read certain scriptures out loud. They would then yell at her with vulgar language. At other times I would be completely unconscious. Several times, I woke up in the fetal position on the floor, crying my eyes out. Judy stated that the bible explains, "the devil has come only but to Steal, to Kill, and to Destroy! The curse is broken tonight, Randy!" Judy declared, "The captivity that Satan had you in; even his very clutches were being disabled by Jesus." The Power of Hell that had been brought into my life was coming to its final *end*.

She continued to pray for deliverance and healing for my mind, my emotions, and my body. She asked God to fill every area that was occupied by these evil spirits with His presence. Two more hours went by. I watched the clock that night in amazement at how hours of time would just disappear instantly.

Later That Night

I looked at my arms when I picked myself up off the floor from a night of wrestling.

"Judy? Look at my arms!" I was so shocked at what I had seen. I had scratch marks that were bleeding from the inside of my elbow all the way down my to my wrists. Judy was convinced that it had been the demons holding on to me and not wanting to let go.

When she was finished I just sat there on the floor, staring at the wall across the room where the clock was. It was now 3:30 a.m.. I was free at last from the powers of a strong delusion. The witchcraft I had been drawn into had brought a strong lie and deception of the truth.

I was so tired that night after my battle for freedom. I explained to Judy once again that I was so sorry for yelling at her, for using such terrible and vulgar language and for calling her those awful names. I walked outside to my car that night seeing the world a whole new way. I stopped and just stared at the trees and the sky. It had a beauty I had never seen before this day. The scales of a multitude of blindnesses had come off my eyes.

My life changed very dramatically that night. I did receive more counseling, healing and regained my liberty over many, many of the months to come, just like the one I had that night in Judy's home. Many were not so dramatic as the first deliverance session, but some were. Life began to turn around over a long period of time.

It Was Finished

If you feel you are in a similar situation, this kind of counseling and deliverance ministry is available in most nearby Christian fellowship Non-Denominational Churches.

To get a list of the Catholic Churches that counsel and to find support in this particular area of the Charismatic Renewal, call 989-684-4640.

If you have any other questions, or are still in need of help, or you are unable to find a place to contact, feel free to write me through my email address:

ElijahsMantle@hotmail.com